For My Family
I Love You All So Much

Time Soldiers®
Book # 1 REX

ISBN: 1-929945-18-3
Library of Congress Cataloging-in-Publication
Data Available

Previously published in 2000 as REX

BiG GUY BOOKS™

Published by BiG GUY BOOKS, Inc.
7750 El Camino Real Suite F
Carlsbad, CA 92009 USA
Printed in Korea

Check out all the NEW STUFF at www.timesoldiers.com

Robert Gould's
REX

Book #1 in the TIME SOLDIERS® Series

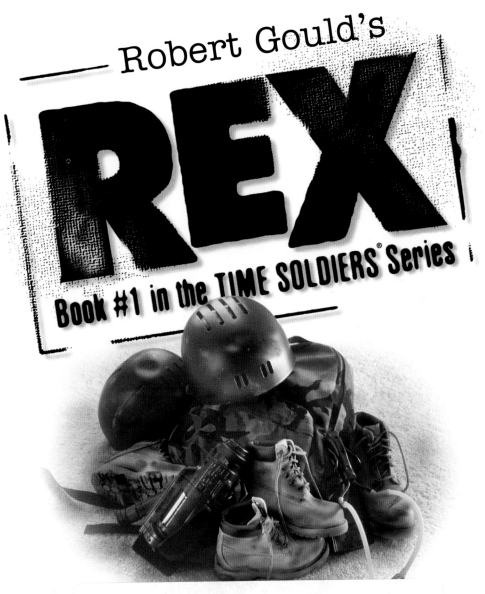

Created and Photographed by Robert Gould
Digitally Illustrated by Eugene Epstein
Written by Robert Gould and Kathleen Duey

The woods smelled like rain. Squirrels and rabbits scattered, startled by the passing bikes.

"I can't wait!" Mikey yelled to his big brother. Rob grinned. He was excited too. In three days they were going camping and exploring with their best friends. They'd saved all summer for camouflage fatigues and packs...even rafts and slingshots.

Suddenly, Mikey braked, his bike skidding sideways. Rob swerved to miss him, trying to focus on the strange swirling light. This couldn't be real. A *dinosaur?* Rob flinched as it lifted its head to look at them.

"Run!" Rob screamed, stumbling backward. They raced for home.

Minutes later, Rob tried to describe the weird swirling trees and the dinosaur. Mom and Dad enjoyed the story...but they didn't believe it.

He finally gave up. "We're going hiking." Rob said. "All six of us." Mikey nodded. "OK, boys," Mom said. "Be home for lunch."

"Jon," Rob whispered into the phone. "Call Mariah. She can call Adam and Bernardo. Meet us at the club house and —"

"What happened?" Jon interrupted.

"Just bring the gear and wear your camouflage." Rob told him. "And hurry."

Rob hung up, giving Mikey the thumbs-up sign. They changed, then checked their equipment. Mikey got out their slingshots. "We might need these," he said.

Rob opened his bottom drawer and took out the old video camera Dad had given him. If nothing he said could convince his parents, getting the dinosaur on *videotape* certainly would.

Half an hour later the six friends stood staring at the swirling tunnel...and two dinosaurs.

"Apatosaurus," Mariah murmured.

"Can we go in there?" Jon whispered.

"We could explore it," Rob said. Adam nodded.

Mikey looked at Rob. "Let's do it!"

Rob and Jon led them forward.

Bernardo hesitated, then followed.

Rob took a deep breath. The air was sweet with the smell of fresh lake water. The forest was so lush, so incredibly clean.

"Apatosaurus," Mariah repeated quietly. "They weighed 30 tons! Scientists argue about whether or not they lived in water."

"They seem to like wading." Rob said. His voice sounded strangely out of place here. It was so quiet he could hear the sound of his own heartbeat.

A rustling of wings overhead made them all whirl around.

Read the Time Soldiers
ADVENTURE JOURNALS at:

www.timesoldiers.com

MOTION SENSOR: LOCKED

10:21AM

RECORDING: ● ◀| ■ |▶ ≫ BATTERY ▭

"What *is* that?" Bernardo asked.

Rob raised the video camera and framed the flying reptile, zooming in to get a good look. It was huge. He glanced at Bernardo. "Those wings must be 20 feet across."

"Quetzalcoatlus," Mariah told them.

"But that doesn't make any sense because—

"Is it dangerous?" Rob asked.

The uncertain look on Mariah's face told him all he needed to know. "Head for the trees!" he shouted, pushing Mikey ahead of him as they all began to run.

MOTION SENSOR: LOCKED

ZOOM: 10X

10:47AM

RECORDING: ● ◀| ■ |▶ ≫ BATTERY ▭

Rob counted helmets. Six. Everyone was safe...so far. The ground trembled, startling him. He turned, raising the video cam.

"Tyrannosaurus Rex," Mariah whispered. "Don't move."

Through the viewfinder, Rob focused on a leg as big as a tree trunk. His heart pounded...

It moved toward them. Adam flinched. "Run!"

Rob grabbed his arm. "No! Don't!!"

"Motion will attract it," Mariah said.

Bernardo was trembling. Jon put a reassuring arm around him. "It'll be OK," he said.

Adam closed his eyes. Mikey stood still as a rock, his fists tightly clenched.

ZOOM OFF

10:49 AM

RECORDING: ○ ◀| ▪ |▶ ≫ BATTERY ▭

The ground shuddered beneath the Tyrannosaur's massive weight as it moved through the brush. Then, abruptly, the dinosaur stopped. Rob heard branches breaking...then a dull tearing sound.

"It's feeding," Mariah whispered. "Its kill must be on the other side of those bushes."

Rob zoomed in for a better look.

"We can't stay this close," Adam said in a shaky voice, stepping back.

Rob turned to grab him, but Adam was already moving away. Bernardo jumped up to follow.

Then, in stunned silence, Rob watched as the T-Rex slowly lifted its huge head...

ZOOM: OFF

10:51AM

RECORDING: ● ◀ ▌ ■ ▐ ▶ ▶▶ BATTERY ▭

"Run!" Jon shouted, shoving at Rob.

Mariah yelled something, but her voice was lost in the thunder of the Tyrannosaur's roar...a sound that made Rob's teeth vibrate. Running was useless. "Climb!" He shouted. "Hide in the trees!"

Mikey found a low branch and started climbing.

Rob followed him, clutching the videocam tightly. Once he and his brother were on a sturdy limb he glanced back. Jon and Adam were in a tree across the clearing. Mariah and Bernardo were closer. They looked terrified.

The T-Rex was staring right at them.

Rob turned the video cam back on and zoomed in. He could see the giant nostrils flare with each breath. Beyond the T-Rex he saw the kill, a small Triceratops. A darting motion caught Rob's eye. He lowered the camera. Two smaller dinosaurs were running through the forest, toward T-Rex's unguarded supper.

"Velociraptors..." Mariah shuddered.

"They're fast," Rob whispered as he pointed. Mikey nodded.

One of the scavengers was already tearing off a big chunk of meat...with needle sharp teeth. As it did, another horrendous roar exploded the air. T-Rex had seen the raptors.

ZOOM: 10X

10:54AM

RECORDING ◉ ◁ ❚ ◼ ❚ ▷ ▷▷ BATTERY ▭

One of them looked up defiantly. The T-Rex attacked, its jaws closing around the raptor's neck. There was a sickening crunch...then an eerie silence.

The Tyrannosaur lifted its head, looking for the other raptor. Rob turned off the camera and scanned the bushes. Where *was* it?

"Rob, watch out!" In the silence, Jon's voice was startling.

"Shhh!" Rob hissed at him.

Then Mikey pointed downward, his face pale. Rob twisted around.

The second Velociraptor scratched wildly at the tree trunk, leaping up, snapping at his foot.

Rob jerked his leg upward, nearly losing his balance. The raptor jumped again...

MEET THE TIME SOLDIERS at:

www.timesoldiers.com

A volley of sharp rocks spattered the tree trunk and the raptor's hide. Angered, it turned to face Mariah and Bernardo standing at the foot of their tree.

It took a leap toward them, then stopped as they reloaded and fired again. Rob heard the rocks hit hard. Shrieking, the raptor spun, then leapt away disappearing into the trees.

That was too close, Rob thought to himself. He lifted the video cam, zooming in to get a final shot of the raptor as it ran away.

Then he swung back around, still looking through the camera and...

ZOOM: MAX

10:58AM

RECORDING: BATTERY

Rob caught his breath.

"Oh no..." Mikey turned. "It sees us."

Rob nodded, lowering the camera.

The Tyrannosaurus wasn't as close as it looked through the zoom lens, but it was much too close for comfort, and it was staring at *them* now. There was only one thing they could do.

"Run for the river!" Rob shouted, scrambling downward. He made sure Mikey was running the right direction, then looked across the clearing. He could see the T-Rex moving through the trees.

Mariah was in the lead. Bernardo had slowed so Mikey could catch up. Jon was running hard, dodging trees and bushes. Rob and Adam followed close behind.

18

Mikey stumbled. Rob glanced back. The T-Rex was getting closer. Suddenly, Jon stopped and loaded a stone into his slingshot.

Rob held his breath as his best friend took careful aim, drew back, then released.

ZZZzzzzzzaaap! The stone struck hard, right between the Tyrannosaur's eyes. Startled, roaring in fury, the dinosaur charged, shaking its massive head.

Jon bolted, leaping fallen logs and diving behind a clump of bushes.

Confused by the mysterious pain, the T-Rex smashed into a huge tree and fell sideways. The ground shook violently.

"Can you see the river?" Jon shouted.

"This way!" Rob yelled.

At the top of the ridge, Rob saw the white foam of rushing water below. Jon jumped, skidding down the muddy bluff. Rob followed. Within seconds, everyone was sliding...

Jon was leaning, guiding his slide like a muddy snowboarder. Rob imitated him...and yelled at Mikey to use his balance. The wild slide was turning into fun. Rob glanced back at the bluff. There was no sign of the Tyrannosaurus.

"We made it!" Jon shouted as the slope leveled out beside the river. Everyone cheered.

"Oh no," Bernardo said.

Rob looked up, then quickly scrambled to his feet.

Staring hungrily at them was the biggest lizard he had ever seen...

"Inflate the rafts!" Rob yelled, searching for a rock. "Hurry!" Seconds later he heard air rushing into the valves. Focusing on the monster-sized lizard, he sighted on its face, then changed his mind. There were no trees here to stop an enraged attack.

He shifted his aim to the beard-like pouch under its jaw. Rob exhaled, then released and reloaded in one smooth motion. The lizard leapt back, startled by the sudden pain. Rob shot a second time...and once more the lizard moved backward.

"Get in!" Mariah was yelling."

"Come on!" Mikey shouted.

Rob backed up, watching the lizard. It flicked its tongue and turned away. Rob ran down the bank and jumped into the second raft.

Jon, Adam and Bernardo were already in the current, heading downstream. The water was cold and swift. Rob paddled quickly, trying to catch up.

"We made it!" Mariah shouted over the roaring water.

Then she screamed...

Rob barely saw the giant rock through the whitewater mist. He dug his paddle in hard, steering the raft to the left. Mariah back paddled. They held their breath as the raft cleared the boulder by mere inches.

The two rafts shot downstream side by side.

"This is so cool," Jon grinned. "It's like we've been transported millions of years back in time."

"I just wish this place made sense," Mariah said as they entered quieter waters.

"We must have come through some sort of time portal," Rob said.

"Has to be," Jon agreed. "We're in prehistoric times."

Mariah frowned. "But some of these animals lived millions of years apart. I don't get it."

"Look," Adam pointed. "Triceratops."

"They belong here," Mariah said. "But the Apotasaurus doesn't and — "

"They look almost tame," Adam interrupted.

ZOOM: 5X

3:54PM

RECORDING: ● ◀▮ ▪ ▮▶ ≫ BATTERY ▭

"They're grazers," Mariah said as the raft rounded a bend in the river. "Not predators."

Mikey scooped up some clear water to drink. It was sweet and cold.

Bernardo pointed. "Apatosaurus?"

"Yeah," Mariah said. "More grazers...but from 77 million years *before* T-Rex."

Rob turned the videocam back on. He knew everyone would be amazed at these tapes when they got home. *If* they ever did.

"Maybe we should go back toward the portal..." Rob began, and then stopped. The others shook their heads. No one was ready to go near the Tyrannosaurus yet.

The forests thinned and the river narrowed as it passed into more arid country. They pulled the rafts ashore in a red sandstone canyon.

"No T-Rex here," Rob said. "No trees."

Mariah shrugged. "No one really knows where they lived."

"We'll tell 'em," Mikey joked. "Forests."

Everyone laughed. "We have to start home," Rob said quietly.

"How?" Bernardo asked.

"Follow the river back to the lake," Jon said.

Rob nodded. "And search for the portal."

"Hey guys!" Mikey called. "Some of those rocks down there sparkle like *gold!*"

"Look!" Adam yelled. "There's a passageway!"

"I'm hungry," Bernardo said quietly. No one answered and he sighed. "I want to go home."

"We all do," Adam said. He led the way. It was strange and beautiful at the same time.

As Mikey walked, he kept stopping to pick up rocks, putting them into his pockets.

Rob walked slowly, thinking. What were they going to do if they couldn't find the portal?

The (Quetzalcoatlus) they had seen at the waterfall was circling above them. "It's just curious," Mikey said.

Mariah nodded. "Like the Triceratops and the Apatosaurus. They've never seen anything like us before."

Learn more about flying reptiles at: **www.timesoldiers.com**

The sun was hot, and Rob was getting tired, when a sparkle in the rock made him blink. He climbed down and picked up a glittering stone.

"It's gold!" he whispered. He opened his hand to show Jon the shiny, yellow metallic rock.

"Gold!" Jon shouted. Everyone gathered to see.

"Look!" Bernardo said. "Here's another piece!"

Mikey grinned. "Are we going to be rich?"

"If I were rich, I'd buy the skateboard store," Rob said.

Jon grinned. "I'd buy a dirt bike and a go-cart!!"

Mariah laughed. "We could give money away to kids who didn't have any!"

They spread out, searching the rocks for more nuggets.

"We have to keep going," Rob reminded them

Mikey frowned. "I bet we could find a lot more gold if we could just stay a little longer . . ."

ZOOM:OFF

RECORDING: ● ◀| ■ |▶ ≫ BATTERY ☐

4:50 PM

"Here," Rob said, handing Mikey the videocam. "Get a shot of me with this!"

Mikey was careful to hold the camera steady as he taped Rob with the gold against the amazing blue of the prehistoric sky.

"We better get going," Jon said.

Rob sighed. "Let's go guys." Adam looked up from the gravel he was sifting. Bernardo stood, dusting off his shorts. Mariah squinted into the sun as they started off.

4:57PM

RECORDING: ● ◀| ■ |▶ ▶▶ BATTERY 🔋

Rob kept the camera on. The scenery changed as they walked, and the river widened again.

"What's that sound?" Bernardo asked.

Rob listened. He shook his head. "A waterfall? The *lake* had a waterfall."

Mikey found a way down the steep ridge... a great short cut through the house-sized boulders.

Everyone followed.

Read the Time Soldier's
ADVENTURE JOURNALS at: www.timesoldiers.com

ZOOM.OFF

5:17PM

RECORDING: ● ◁Ⅰ ■ Ⅰ▷ ▷▷ BATTERY ▭

The waterfall was magnificent, but there was no river and no lake. The water bubbled up from underground springs, and then ran over the cliffs. Below, it roared into a crevasse that must have led to underground caverns and tunnels because the water simply disappeared.

Rob videotaped a huge flower Mariah and Mikey found. She was smiling. "I noticed one of these just inside the portal, when we first came through..."

"I hope we can find it," Rob said wistfully.

"Hey, you guys!" Jon shouted.

Rob stared, astonished. Jon was walking on *nothing!*

"It feels weird, Rob," he laughed. "Try it!"

Rob went next, making sure it wasn't dangerous. It was like wading through an anti-gravity puddle.

"Where's Adam?" Jon asked suddenly. Everyone stopped joking and turned to look around.

"I don't believe it," Bernardo said, pointing. "Look!"

"A Centrosaurus!" Mariah gasped. "A *baby* one!!"

"Is Adam doing what I *think* he's doing?" Mikey asked. "Hey, there's a baby longneck too!"

See Mariah's Fascinating Dinosaur Facts at: **www.timesoldiers.com**

Adam let the Centrosaurus sniff his hand. Then he climbed onto its back.

Everyone watched as Adam and the little dinosaur played, tearing back and forth.

Mikey tossed his pack to Rob, then
ran toward the baby Apatosaurus.

Its mother looked at him closely.
The baby was curious and friendly.

Mikey patted the little
dinosaur. It lowered its
head, and stared into
Mikey's eyes. A moment
later, he straddled its
long neck. When it raised
its head, he slid down
onto its back.

It didn't notice his weight
and followed its mother
up the hill. Mikey rocked
with the dinosaur's gait;
its baggy skin felt cool
against his legs.

On the ridge top, he looked
down at a wide lake. In the
dusk he saw a waterfall at
the far end. A towering forest
grew along the shoreline.

"Rob!" he shouted. "There's
the lake!" He jumped down
and ran toward his friends.

ZOOM: 5X

WARNING: LOW BATTERY!!

RECORDING: ● ◀| ■ |▶ ▶▶ BATTERY

"Can anyone see the portal?" Rob asked as they headed downhill.

"Not yet," Mariah answered. "But it has to be — "

"There!" Jon said. "I think…"

"I see it, too," Mikey said joyfully.

Rob raised the videocam and got a shot of the sunset-colored sparkle in the forest and the watering hole full of dinosaurs. The battery was almost dead. He zoomed in on the trees as the low battery warning sounded. A quick movement startled him…

RECORDING: ◉ ◁| ■ |▷ ≫   FAILURE ▭

WARNING!!

The strange image in the viewfinder made Rob stumble backward. He lowered the camera and peered at the edge of the forest. But it was gone now.

"Rob? Are you all right?" Jon asked.

They took off their packs and threw them in first. It seemed safe. Rob clutched the videocam close to his chest and walked forward...into the portal. He felt a tingling prickle on his skin.

Coming out of the portal, he saw the woods, *their* woods, in the morning sunlight.

Everything was calm and familiar. It still smelled like rain.

"How can it *still be morning?*" Mikey asked.
No one answered.

"Let's get back to the club house," Rob said.
"We have to figure this out."

Jon nodded without saying anything.
They started off. Mariah glanced back.
She blinked, startled.

"Wait you guys! Look, it's...it's..."

"Look at what?" Adam asked.
Mariah blinked, then rubbed her eyes.
Rob frowned. "There's nothing there."
"Let's go," Mikey said.

Adam shrugged his pack higher on his shoulders. "Come on Mariah. You're just tired."

She glanced back once more, then followed the boys up the path.

"We were only gone an *hour?*" Rob kept repeating. It wasn't possible — but somehow, it was true.

"None of our parents will believe this," Jon said.

"The videocam," Rob said. He smiled. "We'll get them together tomorrow and show everyone the tape."

"Good idea," Mariah said.

"And not a single word to any of them until then," said Jon.

"And we never tell any other kids," Mikey added. "It's our secret."

Everyone promised.

It was a perfect plan.

But later, in the
silence of the night...

What happens when T-Rex comes through the portal the next morning? Will the Time Soldiers be able to protect their own neighborhood? Don't miss their next fantastic adventure. For a sneak preview, join them at:

www.timesoldiers.com

Sunday 5:13 A.M. Guess who's coming for breakfast?